"Tales of the 23rd PRECINCT"

Table of Contents

"Tales of the 23rd PRECINCT"

By: Kevin Eleven

Illustration by:
Alton Taylor

http://www.floweredconcrete.net/ (Official Website)

http://floweredconcrete.com (Flowered Concrete Blog)

http://www.booksie.com/Kevin11 (Author Portfolio)

http://amazon.com/author/kevineleven (Author Page)

http://kevinanglade.wordpress.com/ (The Author's Blog)

@floweredconcrete (Instagram) @floweredlit (Twitter)

Flowered Concrete © *kevinanglade@gmail.com

To Samantha, my best friend and loving supporting baby sister. This is not a dedication page but just know that if you see this, I love you more than a brother can ask for. To Mom, I love you. Without your presence, there would be no us.

And to any kid who has ever dreamed of becoming anything but only to have naysayers shut them down. Life is all about obstacles, and detractors will hinder your progression and purpose every step of the way. Be wary of your support system and go out and make all of your dreams a reality. Envision your goals every day and I guarantee you they will be closer than you think...

Dedicated

To my Father for raising me, my sister for being a second mother to me and last but not least my grandmother for teaching me about the right and wrongs of life as they have all passed on...

&

To my big cousin Reginald who bought me my first Harry Potter book at the tender age of 10...

Thank You

Part I: "Crossfires @ 59th & Columbus"

Deborah and Daniel Lane, her husband of five years had just finished celebrating their fifth wedding anniversary. The two had just gotten home to their SoHo apartment. To celebrate, they had went to Cher Maurice's over in Midtown between 33rd and 8th avenue. Lane's detective partner of six years, Luke Fisher had recommended the place to her being that it was in his opinion, the best spot to eat in town. As they settled in, Deborah Lane could now be seen on the sofa with her husband watching a prime time movie on the Cinemax network. As she lied on Daniel's chest, it couldn't have been stressed more that she was currently in a great place. To Lane, it felt wonderful to be just a regular woman for once. Her vigorous job as a burglary Detective in

Brooklyn's 23rd precinct often left her tense, busy

and on edge. But detective Lane never complained,

she truly enjoyed her work. Lane was usually caught

after hours in her cubby double checking files, going

to crime labs, and calling her squad team. If

anyone could compare her to anything,

 many wouldn't have passed on the opportunity to

call her a gym rat. But as she remained in the same

position on Daniel's chest visibly comfortable, she

was truly glad to have had her hair down for once...

   "I love you," she crooned to Daniel in her most

delicate voice.

   "I love you too," said Daniel absentmindedly.

 It was now 11p.m. The movie they had been

watching had just ended and Daniel had now given

his full devoted attention to the evening's nightly segment of ESPN's SportsCenter. As detective Lane rubbed Daniel's chest she suddenly had a change of heart as she pushed him and got up. In the moment that she started for the kitchen to pour herself some wine, Daniel with a perplexed look on his face said,

"What was that for?"

"That's all you men care about nowadays, your damn sports and ESPN," she exclaimed.

Daniel had now walked over and wrapped his arms around her.

"I care about you more," he said in a playful voice.

"Yeah, whatever," she said as she rolled her eyes.

"Hey hun, don't forget Amber is coming this Thursday from California for her open house tour at NYU next weekend. I would pick her up, but I've got a new case and a client that I need to get acquainted with," said Daniel.

"Not a problem," said Lane. "What time does her flight arrive?"

"Five!" he yelled as he made his way towards the bedroom.

This was perfect for detective Lane, she usually had an early start at the precinct around 8 a.m. and often finished her work around four in the evening.

As she propped herself back onto the sofa and began to watch the evening news, her Nextel dispatcher bleeped. Within the moment, she closed her eyes.

The evening had been going so well; her dinner with Daniel, their rare night together in the apartment, she knew this was all about to change the minute

she answered the dispatch. Detective Deborah Lane
was now about to embark into a new burglary case...
Lane pulled out the Nextel phone from her pajamas
and pressed the push-to-talk button.

"Go," she said.

"Was I interrupting something special between
you and Danny boy?" teased Fisher in a playful
voice.

"Oh be quiet Luke," snapped Lane.

"Anyways, what's new?"

"Citibank," he now said seriously.

"The main one on Wall Street has just been
robbed."

"What?" she asked in disbelief.

Detective Lane now stood upright.

"That's what I said as well," he replied.

"But there's so much surveillance and security there."

"How did they do it?" she asked curiously.

"They used C4 explosives to blow out the elevators on the east wing and had one of their guys positioned on the top roof as a guard," said Fisher in a nonchalant manner.

"How did they escape?" said Lane. She was obviously frustrated.

"A news chopper was ushered to the top of the roof by the phony guard and as it landed, the guard pulled out a .40 caliber on the entire news team and in that same exact moment, the bank robbers came out.
From there, one of the news reporters said that they jacked the helicopter," he replied.

"How much did they take?" she now asked.

"North of 5 million," Fisher responded.

"Shit, these assholes may be the same guys who robbed Wells Fargo on Lexington avenue last year," she said.

Lane had longed for the chance to finally nab the crooks. She wasn't assigned that case and they had just gotten away the year before.

"I have no doubt in my mind it's them. Captain Gordon wants the both of us to meet him at Citibank first thing tomorrow," he said.

"No doubt, I'll meet you guys there," said Lane.

"Roger that, see you then," he replied.

And without another word, Detective Lane ended the walkie-talkie conference on her dispatch.

The next day, Detective Lane parked her 2001

Mercedes-Benz adjacent to the Citibank building on Wall Street. As she filled up her parking meter by the sushi cart at the end of the block where she parked her car, she noticed that her partner detective Luke Fisher had just pulled up behind her in his crimson red 98' BMW.

"Morning," he said as he filled up his own meter.

"Morning," she replied.

"Shall we head up?" he asked her as they headed towards the bank's entrance.

"Yes we should, Captain Gordon's already up there," she told him.

Once inside the bank, a young secretary by the name of Stacy Collins told them where to catch an elevator that would lead them to the twelfth floor.

They had to catch one on the west side of the building since the crooks had entirely demolished the elevator system on the east wing. Once they had reached the top, they found Captain Gordon in discussions with a Citibank official about the past night's events. As they approached him, he gave the both of them official police reports of what had transpired the night before.

"C4, assault rifles and semi-automatics. The three suspects were dressed in all black with ski masks and apparently a guard was in on it too," said Gordon. Charles Roberts, who happened to be head of security at the Citibank cut in,

"No disrespect sir, but that impersonator last night definitely wasn't one of our own."

"Then we'll add him to the list of suspects too,"

said Gordon, obviously flustered.

"Is that the news reporter who happened to have her helicopter jacked last night?" Lane asked as she looked past Gordon.

"That most certainly is," Gordon replied as he turned to look at her too.

Without further hesitation, detective Lane walked over to the news reporter who happened to be standing in a corner on the floor alone. The reporter was staring out the glass window as the morning's sun started to rise.

"Excuse me?" Lane asked in a polite voice.

"Are you the news reporter who experienced the unfortunate events last night?" The woman who had kept her still gaze on the sunrise suddenly turned around. She was an attractive woman possibly of

Irish decent in her early thirties with long brown hair, greenish eyes and pearly white teeth. The cream colored trench coat she wore covered a nice black blouse that she had worn beneath it.

"Yes I am," she answered.

"Toni McHale," she said as she shook Detective Lane's hand.

"Detective Deborah Lane."

"Nice to meet you detective," she replied.

"Did you manage to get a good look at the suspects. Any faces, tattoos, scars, anything that would make them recognizable?"

"No, but as they were about to fly off in our helicopter they said that they would reconvene at a hotel," she said.

"Do you remember the name of the hotel in which

they spoke of?" asked Fisher as he had now made

his way over to the two women.

"No, I don't, but as they got in the chopper three

of the crooks were obviously furious with the guy

who had asked," said Toni.

"Why?" asked Lane.

"Because my whole news team was there and they

knew him saying that could lead to info for the

BKPD's investigation," replied Toni.

"I wonder what would cause a professional

criminal to ask a stupid question such as that?"

asked Fisher.

"This one was young," said Toni.

"He stood about six foot three but by his voice

and the way he spoke, he couldn't have been any

older than twenty one or twenty two."

"What about the guard? Did you get a good look at him?" asked Lane.

"Yes, he was a Caucasian male in his early thirties, and he held us up while the crew came out. We couldn't see his eyes because he had on a dark pair of shades and a baseball cap to cover his head," said Toni.

"Well thanks for the heads up to say the least," said Lane.

"No problem, it was my pleasure," said Toni. As they met Captain Gordon in the front of the bank's lobby they all vowed to meet up at headquarters after their midday lunch break. Later in the afternoon, Detective Fisher found Lane in the squad room. It was apparent that she had cut her lunch break short to check out the bank's surveillance tape on the heist.

"Any clues so far?" asked Fisher.

Fisher often admired Lane's constant and persistent nature. He had often felt that he was kind of laid back when approaching his work. Lane's tenacious work ethic always led to things getting done, and cases being solved. She wasn't three detective rankings above him for nothing...

"I've noticed one thing," she said as she broke his train of thought.

"But I'm not sure if it will account for anything later on."

"What is it?" asked Fisher.

"The moment these three guys leave the elevator, one of them makes an army salute right into the camera," Lane replied.

As Lane said this, she rewound the tape multiple times where the criminal saluted to the camera as they made their elevator exit.

"This one thinks he's a celeb huh?" Fisher said as he watched the video.

"Just a cocky asshole," muttered Lane under her breath.

"If there's one thing we can say about him it's that he must be the youngster of twenty one or twenty two," said Fisher.

"That's what I was thinking," Lane replied.

"Boy, this kid has got a lot to learn," said Fisher, as he shook his head in amusement.

In just that moment, Captain Gordon walked in. Behind him were other members of the squad team. The entire room went silent.

"Ladies and gents, we're dealing with four notorious criminals," he said.

"Their plans of attack occur about once a year. They rob the biggest banks in the city and leave no traces of even a fingerprint behind. Their leader goes by the name of Zach Richards. Forty five years old, British Male, came to the U.S. at the age of nineteen as a Columbia University undergrad. He used to work as an investment broker on Wall Street so he knows all about the economy and the cities federal shares. There are questions to whether if this group involved was of his doing because a British accent wasn't heard and there hasn't been a single trace of this guy in about a year," said Gordon.

"Maybe he went back to the U.K." said Fisher in

a parody of a London accent.

"The poor bloke couldn't live up to the American dream."

Smirks and snickering had then ascended from most of the members in the room.

"That is a strong possibility Fisher, thank you for that resounding moment of entertainment," replied Gordon sarcastically.

"Have any of you found anything? Any recent discoveries?" he added.

"I was just reviewing the tape of the heist Captain. It turns out that one of the robbers did a military salute gesture after stealing the money and my thoughts are that he's a novice in the burglary game," reported Lane off of her typed analysis.

Fisher happened to have a police report as well and said, "Yesterday, after talking to Ms. Toni McHale of the 11p.m. channel 3 news, one of the robbers had asked if they were going to reconvene at a hotel. My guess is that the guy who asked the question happens to be the same asshole who performed the gesture in front of the elevator's surveillance camera."

"I can't imagine him being past his early twenties as well," Lane added.

"Listen! These bastards are clever. They only perform jobs about once a year and they obviously do a bit of research and have concise prior knowledge on the banks that they hit. Now we don't know any of their identities, but help me God when I say we're going to bring them down. Be aware, although it's not guaranteed, these crooks could be

working for Zach Richards so I want you all well

informed and acquainted with who he is. Go out, do

your homework, and try to find me as many leads as

possible! Ok, dismissed!" said Gordon.

One by one the squad room emptied as each

detective went out into the corridors.

"Hey Deb, I'm thinking we should go check out

Cheknov, you know he used to be an arms dealer

and I just know parole is gonna get him talking,"

said Fisher.

"Yeah, but due to his court ordered community

service he won't be working the hot dog cart until

Tuesday. In the meantime we can work here and see

if we can find any valuable information on these

guys," said Lane.

"Thank God I've got you for a partner Deb, I forget to use my head sometimes," said Fisher with a sigh. Detective Lane suppressed a giggle, she was glad that Luke Fisher was her partner; she often felt as if he had given her a kind of balance. If he was as determined and as strong minded as her, in no way would their chemistry have worked...

Tuesday had now arrived and detective Fisher picked up Deborah Lane in front of her SoHo condo. Today they were going to 32nd and eighth. Across the street from Madison Square Garden, Demetri Cheknov, a former Russian arms dealer happened to sell hot dogs and other goods at a food stand. Cheknov had done seven out of a ten year sentence at the Ithaca Federal Prison in upstate New York.

Now that he was on parole, he claimed that he no

longer knew or cared on what was happening in the

streets. But once a street hustler, always a hustler...

"Cheknov, how's it going man?" asked Fisher as

the two of them approached him.

Cheknov was a Russian ex-hustler in his mid-

fourties.

He stood a little over six feet with a strong physique

intact. His mullet hairstyle was of a sandy brown

color and he had grown a full beard from when they

had last seen him. The fact that he was a hairy

specimen gave him the luxury of hiding his beady

brown eyes. There were talks that in his day he often

did coke so he looked now as if he was in his mid-

fifties.

"Oi, vhat do you vant?" asked Cheknov. For him,

any moment seeing BKPD cops meant pain and distress.

"I aven't seen nozzing," he said in his thick Russian accent.

"C'mon, two cops can't grab a bite while talking to an old friend?" asked Fisher.

"I'd like a hot dog with no relish, make that two as a matter of fact. One for me and my good friend Deb here."

"No thanks, I'm not hungry," she said.

Cheknov didn't take his eyes off them.

"Make that one then," said Fisher as he leaned his forearm against the cart.

"Vhat do you vant?" he asked again.

"What do you know about Citibank being robbed on Wall Street last Friday?" asked Lane.

"I know nozzing," he pressed.

"Give me something!" Lane demanded.

After a few seconds of intense gazing between the two, he finally said,

"Zere's a new guy out ere on zeese streets."

"Well? Give me a name!" she barked.

"I don't know it!" he said.

Cheknov was really getting annoyed now.

"The lady asked for a name Cheknov, what's the name?" pressed Fisher.

"Ow many times do I ave to tell you!?" he exclaimed.

Detective Lane knew when someone was being honest with no intention of suppressing critical information.

"Ok go on," she urged him.

"Anyways," said Cheknov.

He shot Fisher a dirty look as he said it.

"Zere's a new ustler, I forget zhe name but e's an Aussie crook who just started on 'is share of crimes in the city. Ee's a very good friend of Zach Richards. The word going around town is zhat zhey're starting to build an international plot to rob the big banks in zhe biggest markets of zhe world. Zis Aussie 'as 'is own crew back 'ome but I zink he came over to lead Richards' crew in 'is absence."

"Where's Richards?" asked Lane.

For one thing, I know ee's out of zhe country. If zhere were any signs of him resurfacing, my people would've told me," said Cheknov.

"What about the other crooks involved? Know their names?" asked Fisher.

"Two of zhem used to be in the navy, but after zheir tour of duty in Europe back in 1998 zhey settled on banks and armored car robberies. One of zhem goes by zhe name David Fredette, zhe ozher by zhe name of Isaac Rivers. And if I'm not mistaken, Isaac 'as a little brother and it's only a matter of time before ee follows 'is brother into zhe business."

"Well," said Fisher, "thanks for your help in supplying dime to the 23rd precinct."

Without another word, he started to walk off. Detective Lane thanked Cheknov and assured him that his name would not circulate throughout the streets after he had violated one of the biggest street codes known to crime.

Two days later, detective Lane was in her office with Fisher and Gordon discussing the case. They now had narrowed down their choice of suspects. As they

spoke in frantic matters about the case, the door to

Lane's office was knocked...

"Come in," said Gordon in his deep usual tone.

Detective Frank Matthews of the homicide

department had just walked in. He was an African-

American senior detective with a grizzly black

caesar, dark chin hair and a worn look on his

blank face. Matthews was in his early

sixties, but like Gordon, looked young for his age.

He rarely came into the burglary department

however, but when he did he usually came looking

for Gordon.

"You called for me James?" he asked.

"Yes," Gordon replied hastily.

"I need you and Detective Alvin out looking for

this guy."

He threw some old photo documents and

newspaper clippings at Detective Matthews.

"His name is Ron Mercer, you'll find him in the

Bedford-Stuyvesant area of Brooklyn. Apparently

he's plotting a murder on a former dealer who

snitched on one of his employees a few years back. I

need you two to track him down ASAP!"

"Not a problem," he said in a grumble. And from

there, Matthews left without another word.

"As for you guys," he said as he turned his

attention once more to Lane and Fisher.

"You two have assembled all the pieces that have

led us to the possible suspects, now try your best to

ring them in. Keep me posted with what you find."

"No problem, we're on it sir," replied Lane.

Captain Gordon shook the both of their hands and

left.

"I'm going to scram, I've got a T.V. dinner and a wife whose calling my name," said Fisher as he gave a mild yawn.

Detective Deborah Lane looked at the big clock just above the office door.

"Yeah, I have to head out too. Danny's niece is flying in from California and I promised to go pick her up."

"Cool, see you tomorrow then. Same time, same place," said Fisher.

"Yep, see you," said Lane as she typed some last minute details of the case into her personalized station desktop computer.

Luke Fisher left, and Deborah Lane soon departed not long after him. When she decided to take a look at the clock, she noticed that it was

4:30pm, and that she still had about thirty minutes

until Amber's flight arrived. It was only five minutes

later when Lane found herself on the Long Island

Expressway merging onto the Grand Central and

then getting off at the Van Wyck which led her

directly to JFK.

She now arrived at the airport at approximately

5:30p.m.

As she got out of her car to look for her niece,

someone from the baggage claim within the airports

entrance screamed "Aunt Debby, Aunt Debby!!"

Before she knew it, Daniel's niece Amber was

wrapping her in a big hug.

"How are you?" Lane asked.

"I'm fine, I'm so happy to be here," exclaimed

Amber. Amber was a beautiful girl of around the

age of seventeen. She had long jet black hair that

lied neatly on her back and she wore a Hollister

designer t-shirt, navy blue cardigan, blue

Levi jeans, and black air Jordan sneakers.

"Are you ready to check out NYU?" asked Lane

enthusiastically.

"Oh of course!"

"I'll be going there most likely, it's my first choice,"

she added confidently.

"Let me get your bags, you can go ahead and sit

in the car for a minute," said Lane.

As Lane approached the revolving cycle of bags, she

happened to pick up a bag that she thought was

Amber's. However, someone else had grabbed the

suitcase at the exact same time. A young man who

happened to be in his early twenties.

"I'm sorry," said Lane. "I thought it was my

niece's."

"Don't be," he said with a charming smile on his face.

"I'm Jason, but you could call me J.R." he said as he extended his right hand.

Detective Lane took his hand and shook it.

"Deborah," she said.

"You need any help with that?" he asked, as Lane removed Amber's bag amongst others from the revolving cycle.

Lane peered into his face. He was a good looking young black man in his early twenties. He stood between six foot two to six foot four. He had bright brown eyes, a strong physique for someone his age with a light mustache and beard to top it off. He was surely handsome but just a kid. Lane thought she must've been at least eleven years older than him.

"No, it's ok I got it," she said.

"J.R.!" called a man from behind him.

"Well it was nice meeting you," he said with another charming smile.

"Same," she said as she returned his smile.

As J.R. walked away, detective Lane saw him greet a man of about is height with a British accent. As they met and J.R. gave the man his suitcase, they both happened to slap each other five and then gave each other a quick army salute gesture. They then laughed and chatted as they left the lobby.

Detective Lane wondered, could he be the Zach Richards that everyone was talking about?

And this kid, Jason or J.R. as he liked to call himself.

Could that R in his initials stand for Rivers as in the younger brother of the suspected Isaac Rivers? There wasn't time to ask any questions. Detective Lane quickly ushered Amber to the car and threw her stuff in the trunk.

"Aunt Debby, what's going on?" she asked.

"I'll explain everything later hun, right now I've got some business to tend to," said Lane frantically. J.R.'s parked car ahead of them had just pulled off. Lane, not wanting to tailgate too close gave them a moment before she herself pulled off. Luckily for her, J.R. had led her back onto the Grand Central, then back onto the Long Island Expressway as they entered midtown of Manhattan no less than half an hour later.

As detective Lane continued to tail the car, it soon

came to a complete halt in front of the Hudson

Hotel on west 58th street, a block off of 59th and

Columbus Circle.

Lane, not wanting to attract attention to herself

waited for them to cross the street. Once they

crossed, she parked her car further down the block

so that it wouldn't look suspicious.

"Do me a favor will you sweetheart?" she told

Amber.

"Look into my glove compartment, and in there

you'll find a set of binoculars."

Amber quickly opened the compartment and thrust

the binoculars into Lane's hands. Lane had now

turned around from the driver's seat, binoculars in

hand and pressed her eyes hard against them. In

order to hear the conversation, she had rolled down

her driver's window.

J.R. was now bringing the British man's luggage to the front entrance. Another man with a pair of shades had just come to meet them outside.

"Richards," said the man in an Aussie accent.

"Flight was ok I hope?"

Richards smiled as he shook his hand.

"Never been better," replied Richards in his natural British accent.

"Come on gents, let's go discuss business inside." And in a matter of about three seconds, they all disappeared as they headed into the lobby's entrance. So *this* was Zach Richards, thought Lane. And without a doubt J.R. was young inexperienced Jason Rivers. The Hudson hotel apparently was the spot that the criminals had met to discuss their plans. But it had only been a week since Citibank on Wall Street was hit. Were they planning another heist so soon? Lane had many things to tell the squad team in the morning but her main priority now was getting Amber home.

"Come on," she said.

"I think you've had enough for one day, I'm sure Daniel can't wait to see you."

The next day in the squad room, Lane had recounted all of the prior evening's events to Captain Gordon, Luke Fisher and the rest of the burglary investigations department.

"So Zach Richards was away. Just as I had expected," thought Gordon aloud as he rubbed a rarely sported scruffy black beard.

"Yeah, J.R. picked him up," Lane added.

"Man, this kid Rivers is really an all-pro perennial rookie."

"He'll be the reason why we take these guys down," said Fisher in an amused tone.

"One thing is for sure, Cheknov was right. The unidentified Australian man was leading the crew in Richards' absence," said Lane.

"And now that he's back, there's no telling what could happen," added Fisher.

"Tomorrow, I want that entire hotel surrounded. These guys are probably thinking of striking again real soon and we're not going to let that happen!" said Gordon.

"I want you all at the Hudson first thing in the morning. Do I make myself clear? Dismissed!"

Everyone had started filing out one by one in the squad room. Saturday was shaping up to be an intense day. It was now 4p.m. which meant that detective Lane's day was over. When detective Lane reached home, she found Daniel already home from work playing scrabble with Amber in the living room.

"Who's winning?" she asked.

"I'm kicking Uncle Danny's butt!" she laughed.

Daniel started to chuckle "No you're not, I'm just getting warmed up," he said as he contemplated his next choice of word.

As Detective Lane took a can of ginger ale from the fridge and watched Daniel and Amber's game from the kitchen, her Nextel dispatcher started to beep. Resorting to her natural instincts, she quickly picked up the dispatch and said,

"Go!"

"Detective, it's Gordon, get down here to 33rd

between liberty pronto! They've hit the Federal

Reserve Bank!!" he yelled.

"I'm on my way," she said.

 Detective Lane moved so fast that she had forgot to

tell either Daniel or Amber for her reasons of

leaving. There wasn't enough time anyway.

"They've got a lot of balls," she thought aloud as

she was already half way to the crime scene.

The Federal Reserve Bank was one of the nation's

twelve Federal Government banks in the country.

Conviction of this crime would most certainly mean

life in prison. "*Did they really think that they could

get away with that?*" thought Lane as her car came

to a screeching halt right in front of the bank.

"Lane, over here!" said Gordon.

Fisher had just come from inside the bank, as he approached them he said, "They took somewhere between 20-25 million. They're long gone."

"How'd they escape?" asked Lane.

"Must've used a getaway car," Fisher replied.

"No way," said another cop who happened to be filing an official police report close by.

"What about the subway?" asked Lane.

"Well what about it?" asked Fisher curiously.

"The 2 train goes to Columbus Circle," said Lane.

"So?" stressed Fisher.

"So, these guys are going back to the Hudson. They knew this job would be one of their biggest ones yet, and that the subway would be their best means of escape."

"I think you're on to something Lane, let's get down there," demanded Gordon.

"No captain, have all the guys surround the hotel that way if we don't track them down from below, you guys will have them trapped up top," said Lane.

"Great, let's move out," yelled the captain.

Five minutes later detective Lane had parked her car by the 34th street Penn Station train station. She and Fisher quickly made their way into the subway and found themselves on the 2 train platform. Once they got on the train, they took it straight to the 59th street and Columbus stop. As they got off the train they quickly scanned the scene; the crooks were nowhere to be found.

"It's your call Deb, should we wait around a bit

longer? Or should we head straight for the hotel?" asked Fisher.

Deborah Lane hated when she had to make pressured decisions that could affect a critical outcome.

"Let's go to the hotel, we're not far off from it anyway."

As Lane and Fisher took the stairs which would lead them to the A,E,D, and B train platform, she decided something on the spot.

"C'mon," she yelled.

Lane had started to break into a run.

"What is it?" panted Fisher as he tried to keep up with her.

"The E train," she said as they continued to run. "It goes to Columbus Circle as well. How much do you want to bet that they took that train instead,

knowing that the 2 route at 59th station would be a

hot commodity stacked with cops."

Detective Lane and Fisher zigzagged and shoved

their way through a packed tunnel of people. They

finally reached the end of the corridor which pointed

directions to the E train that led to uptown and

Queens. As Lane and Fisher made their way down a

pair of steps she happened to see a smirking Jason

Rivers and the other members of the heist crew with

big duffel bags strapped to their backs.

"Police!" she cried.

In that precise moment the suspects broke into a

run down the platform unto the next stairway they

happened to come across. The two detectives

pushed and shoved more people out of the way as

they ran after them. As they went up the stairs that

the criminals had taken a second earlier, the crooks

were nowhere to be found. The moment they went

back down the stairs they noticed that they had

simply crossed over to the opposite side of the

platform. Isaac Rivers didn't waste a fraction of a

second, and quickly pulled out his assault rifle. As

they all began to pull out their artillery, civilians left

and right broke out into a panic and headed for

cover. The New York City 59th and Columbus Transit

Authority station had now become an underground

warzone. All hell broke loose as fear and panic filled

the air. A few civilians were caught in the crossfire

and were severely hurt. Six or seven citizens were

probably dead in the heat of fire.

Detective Lane hid behind one of the platforms large

poles while Luke Fisher sat behind a fragmented

bench reloading his .40 caliber glock.

"We need to get these assholes away from here!"

he said.

"The longer we stay down here, the more

opportunities there will be for people to get hurt!!"

"I've already paged for backup!" cried Lane over

the sound of flying bullets from behind the pole.

As she said this, she managed to hit one of them in

the chest.

Down he went...the Australian crook happened to

send another shot down Lane's way. As she ducked

behind her pole for cover, she saw the bullet zoom

past her head. She was extremely lucky in that

moment...The police backup had now arrived as

they infiltrated the platform. Someone had

squeezed a slug right into the center of Zach

Richards's head. Detective Lane knew that as soon as

she had seen him fall to where the tracks of the train

lied invisibly to her naked eye that he was dead...The

Aussie crook, however, was in the midst of preparing

to fire his next round at Fisher who's rear head was

exposed behind the bench when detective Lane

popped him twice in the chest. In an instant he hit

the ground. It was definitely a close call...

Another bank robber who had not been identified

but happened to be a mid-thirties Caucasian male

pulled out a semi-automatic from his bag. He was a

second away from completely removing it when a

bullet was lodged into his right hand which was now

bleeding profusely... The man yelped with pain...

"Bulls-eye," said Fisher from behind the bench as he

had now switched to a .9 millimeter.

In the midst of civilians running and screaming for their lives, Lane saw Jason Rivers fleeing up the stairs. Rivers had ditched his bag and was apparently saving himself.

Lane quickly ran up her opposite side of the platform to chase after him. As she went up the stairs she saw him exit the subway turnstile.

"Freeze!" she screamed.

Rivers pulled out his .45 and squeezed out four shots. Lane ducked and missed the attempts. She quickly took the northwest 59th and eighth avenue exit and met him outside. As Rivers tried to make his escape down the street in a run, two cop cars pulled up and surrounded him. Rivers then quickly went in the opposite direction towards a dark narrow alley. Four more squad cars pulled up to face him.

He then quickly dodged behind a dumpster.

"I give up!" he yelled.

As he got up from behind it, he reached for his back pocket to pull out yet another gun, a .50 pistol but it never happened...As calm as the night, bullets from left to right quickly ripped through the chest of Jason Rivers in the glow of the moonlit sky...

He was lifeless before he hit the ground...As an onslaught of cops and detective Lane crowded the suspect, they peered into the face of the money hungered youth...In the hard knock streets of New York City, the stories often ended this way...Fisher was now seen in the alleyway catching up to his partner. He was sporting a nasty gash under his right eye and a bloody lip.

"The Isaac Rivers bitch got physical with me, he tried to make an escape after his semi-automatic ran out of clips. But I think I'm doing better than him at the moment. I pistol whipped him with my .40 and so he's got a broken jaw now," said Fisher with a smug look.

Isaac, and the Caucasian male shot in the right hand who later turned out to be a criminal by the name of Terry Skyles were captured by the police. Richards and the Australian man who was later identified as Matt Weston were now dead just below them on the E platform. Captain Gordon was moving through the congested crowd of policemen and injured civilians who happened to get caught in the underground crossfires.

"Great job," he told them as he made his way

through a do-not-cross yellow police tape.

"Are these people going to be ok, cap?" asked Lane as she pointed to the injured citizens.

"Yes, they will, and we have the both of you to thank for that," he said with a smile.

"Just doing our job cap," said Fisher as he swooped in to take his credit.

Detective Lane was just glad it was over, what a crazy seven days it had been for her. And now that she and Fisher had wrapped up another case filled with absurd proportions, Lane could now head back home to her niece and husband as she was hopeful to join them in a game of scrabble. The simplistic thought of the matter beat running through underground train platforms having life or death shoot outs any day...

Two weeks later however, Luke Fisher and his wife Jennifer happened to be watching a pay-per-view movie in his Canarsie, Brooklyn apartment when his Nextel dispatcher went off...

"What now?" he thought. It was late Saturday night, and he was off the clock...

"Yes?" he said.

"Fisher, its Gordon," said the Captain.

"What's up cap?" Fisher asked.

"Jacob Fisher's dead," he said.

"Jake? You mean my br—"

"Brother, yes... I'm really sorry," replied the Captain.

Luke Fisher however couldn't hear the words from the captain that came after. He had just went completely numb...When Fisher and Lane had went out to solve even the most heinous acts of the city's criminals, to them, it always made some sort of

sense. But in a city as cold-blooded and vengeful as

New York and its borough's often were, none of it

ever really made sense at all...

Part II: "Misguided Justice" (Strangers, Brothers, Detectives)

Detective Fisher was in a daze. He felt as if someone had knocked the wind out of him. As he managed to look at the three gunshot wounds upon the fractured skull of his dead brother lying on the sofa, he somehow managed to fight back tears. Detective Frank Matthews whom Fisher hadn't known too well but had obviously recognized from the homicide department tried to console him.

"We're going to find out who did this to him Fisher, mark my words," he said.

"I know we hadn't seen eye to eye recently but he was still my brother," said Fisher.

"I understand," said Matthews. He then continued "That's why I was eager to take this case. Homicide is my field of expertise and I have always had the upmost respect for you Fisher."

"I truly appreciate that Matthews. He did 8 years for a drug bust back in 93' and had just been released from sing sing," said Fisher in an unusually dry voice that didn't resemble his own.

As they waited for the medical examiner to arrive Matthews took one last hard look at the dead body of the lifeless Jake Fisher.

"You know, this is it for me," said Matthews as he peered out of the apartment window.

"What is?" asked detective Fisher.

"I'm sixty five now, and I'll be getting my pension real soon. It's time for me to call it quits, but I thought nothing would be better than helping out a detective in whom I truly respect before hanging it up."

"That means a lot to me Matthews, but if you'll

excuse me I'm going outside to see if the medical examiner has arrived."

"Go right ahead," said Matthews.

"I'm going to browse around some more to see if the suspect might've left anything of value," he added.

As both men nodded in agreement, Fisher left the apartment and stood outside of the buildings entrance.

In that moment he quickly took out a cigarette and began to self-indulge in his thoughts. As he looked around, he quickly absorbed the setting of the Bedford-Stuyvesant housing. At one point, he himself was headed down the same path as the current criminals and drug dealers of the neighborhood. At the age of twenty-two, after a near death experience, he had finally decided that enough was enough and that a hustler's lifestyle wasn't for him.

As Fisher exhaled from his cigarette, he thought on how his brother, released from prison earlier in the year had decided to turn his life around. Fisher would forever admire his late brother for this. The one problem was that it had been a little too late. Fisher took one last puff of his cigarette and was in the midst of extinguishing it with his foot when Captain Gordon of the 23rd precinct on Parkside avenue had arrived.

"How are you holding up?" he asked.

Fisher had pangs of anxiety, he hadn't slept in days, and to his dismay, had found out that his brother had been murdered.

"I've been better," he said, in one final exhale of

cigarette smoke.

"This is Paul Sanders by the way, our medical examiner," said Gordon.

Dr. Sanders then extended an arm, both men shook hands.

"Sorry to hear about your brother," he said in a deeply compassionate manner.

"It's alright, thanks for the concern," said Fisher mutually.

Without another word Sanders left the two men facing each other while he made strides towards the apartment.

In that moment, the chilly November wind swept up the leaves and blew them violently in front of the housing project. It was a while before either men spoke.

"Look Fisher, if there's anything I can do please don't hesitate to ask," said Gordon in a brisk manner.

"I do have one request," said Fisher.

"Shoot," fired Gordon.

"I'd love to have detective Deborah Lane on the case with me. I know she isn't part of the homicide department as well as I for that matter, but she is a hard-boiled detective that hasn't failed in any case that we've ever done. I need her," said Fisher.

"You do know that Matthews won't be too happy with the matter but consider it done," said Gordon.

"No disrespect to Matthews cap, he's one of the best, but I've never worked with him and for a case that I consider extremely personal, past chemistry with the likes of Ms. Lane will be important," said

Fisher.

"I completely understand," Gordon responded.

"Well, I'm going home. I promised Jennifer that I
would be at the apartment early tonight. Lately I've
been stressed and now having to deal with this she's
really worried about me," said Fisher.
Captain Gordon didn't hesitate once.

"Get some rest," he advised.

"If anything comes up I'll be sure to ring your cell,"
he assured Fisher.

Without further hesitation, Fisher quickly got into
his red 98' BMW and took off. As he crossed
Flatlands avenue on the way to his Canarsie condo
on East 54th, he couldn't help but think that his
brother's death was his fault. After Jake had been
released from prison earlier in the year, he had come

to Luke asking for a place to live. Luke wasn't sure
that his brother had changed and thought better of
it. After turning his brother down, they hadn't
spoken since March. The least he could do now in
respect to his memory was find his killer.

The crimson red 98' BMW had now come to a
complete halt in front of his apartment complex. As
Fisher rummaged his key into the lock and opened
the door he noticed that his wife Jennifer had been
waiting for him all along within their living room.

"I'm so glad you're home, anything at all?" she
asked concerned.

"No, the medical examiner should have some
findings for us tomorrow. Tomorrow is the first
official day of the case," said Fisher calmly.

"Would you like anything sweetheart?" she asked.

"No, I picked up some tea along the way. I think I'm just gonna go to bed," he said.

The next day, Fisher arrived at the 23rd precinct and managed to engage himself in a rapid discussion with detective Lane. Matthews was there as well but wasn't too thrilled about another detective being on the case. As the trio narrowed down the list of possible informants and leads for the case, medical examiner Paul Sanders walked into the homicide office.

Sanders had a list of files and papers jammed in between the palm of both hands.

"I noticed some things last night that I thought I would share," he said.

"Talk to us Sanders, what do you got?" Lane

responded.

"From last night's investigation while working with coroner Murray, it turns out that the killer had gloves and used some kind of powerful object to fracture the victim's right side of the skull.
We couldn't find any finger prints but we're leaning heavily towards objects such as a hammer or bat that may have been used to brutally beat the victim. The suspect had either opened the window or it was already open, but we think he used that as a decoy to fool anyone who'd be investigating the crime," said Sanders.

"Anything else Dr. Sanders?" asked Fisher earnestly.

"That's all we have for now, but if anything comes up, I'll be sure to have you come to the lab," he said.

"Thanks Sanders, we'll keep in touch," added Matthews.

"Not a problem, if there's anything please don't hesitate," he said.

The three of them were left alone as Dr. Sanders headed towards the medical department.

"Let's get out and hit the streets, time to start pressing the drug peddlers and arms dealers in NYC," ordered Matthews.

"No disrespect detective Matthews but I think the first action would be for us to talk to Jake's former friends, associates, and anyone he's been in contact with over the past few years. Besides, the city landscape has changed and many of the dealers Jake used to mess with are no longer around," interjected Lane.

"I don't tell you how to do your job Ms. Lane so please don't tell me how to do mine," snapped Matthews.

"Listen, if there's anyone who would be a benefit to us, I would say it would be his girlfriend. Her name's Tanya Watson. Lives on Beverly road right off of Flatbush, she knew all of his friends, where he worked, they were often spotted together, she's a start," said Fisher.

"Then let's quickly get over there then, we're moving too slow," said Lane.

Fisher couldn't help but think on why he deeply admired Lane. They both had been burglary detectives for about six to seven years now, and he knew that if there was anyone who was as passionate to solving the case as him, it was definitely Lane...

Once they had reached the front door, Lane quickly

rapped her knuckles against the apartment.

"Who is it?" replied a somber woman's voice

from inside.

"BKPD," said Matthews.

"We'd like talk to you, open up!" added Lane.

The woman quickly opened the door. After letting

them in, she quickly looked at detective Fisher and

burst into tears.

"You look just like him," she said.

"Nice to see you too Ms. Watson," replied Fisher

awkwardly.

"I can't take it!" she said, in between big heavy

sobs.

"Listen, we were wondering if you could give us

some names in regards to who Jake hung around with or his last whereabouts before the unfortunate event," said Fisher.

Tanya tried to collect herself as she sniffled on her couch.

"Well, he had just gotten a job at Kings Plaza mall off the Belt Parkway," she said.

"And what exactly did he do while working there?" asked Lane.

"He was a janitor. My baby cleaned windows and mopped floors.

It wasn't much but it was one of the few jobs he managed to find after being a convicted felon in prison," Tanya said.

"Any places he liked to go on his downtime?" asked Fisher.

"Yeah, he often went to Jibb's, a pool hall located

between Bedford and Ocean. He used to chill with

Smoke, Jeff, and Trey," she said, in the midst of her

sniffle.

"Well thanks for your cooperation and patience, if

we need any more info or testifying in court we'll be

in touch," said Matthews.

"How come you're asking me all these questions?

You know, for someone who happened to be your

brother you barely knew anything about him. He

talked about you constantly. He really wanted to

repair the relationship that you two once had,"

exclaimed Tanya.

Detective Luke Fisher sighed. With one hand

grasped firmly on her door knob he calmly said, "If

we need anything or something comes up, we'll be

68

in contact."

And so, they quickly left Tanya's apartment. As they

headed towards Kings Plaza mall, Fisher couldn't

help but think upon what Tanya had said. She was

right, he was a stranger and after his brother's

incarceration he barely knew anything about him.

Fisher now believed that his brother had changed

for the better but it was too late to recreate their

once close bond. As they arrived at Kings Plaza they

quickly approached a security guard in the front

lobby.

"Excuse me, detective Fisher of BKPD. These

are detectives Lane and Matthews. We're looking for

whoever that happens to be in charge of all the

custodians here," said Fisher.

"Oh, then I guess you'd be looking to speak to Mr.

DeMarco. He's the head of the custodian faculty here," answered the guard.

"Where can we find him?" asked Lane.

"Go straight down this floor and make a left at the end. His office is room 115," said the guard.

As they walked down the first floor of the mall, they had to avoid all the shoppers passing by who were running in and out of stores with clothing apparel and valuables. Thanksgiving happened to be two days away and it appeared as if people were doing some unusual early Christmas shopping.

When they reached DeMarco's office they were surprised to see that the door was open. They walked inside but apparently Mr. DeMarco was on his way out.

"Come back another time, I'm going to lunch," he

said.

Mr. DeMarco was in the act of putting on his coat when Fisher suddenly cut in.

"Lunch can wait Mr. DeMarco. What do you know about the murder of Jake Fisher your employee?" said Fisher.

"Good lord no!! Jake?!" he asked bewildered. He quickly returned behind his desk and propped himself back unto his chair.

"He was murdered late Saturday night, we found him early Sunday morning," said Matthews. Mr. DeMarco repetitively shook his head in a fashion of disbelief.

"Jake, Jake, Jake. A good man, a good man," he said somberly.

"I saw his potential. He was trying to get back on

his feet. I think I'm the only one who was willing to hire him with the previous track record he had. Jake had great articulation and plus he carried himself well. A very ambitious man I would say, he wanted to be a motivational speaker to the youth as a way of shying them away from violence and staying off the streets. He used this job to make money in order to get back on his feet."

"Anything else about Jake that you can tell us?" asked Lane.

"We really didn't talk about much outside of work but I know that on Fridays he'd always get real excited. Once closing came, he always went to that pool hall between Ocean and Bedford."

"Jibbs?" asked Fisher curiously.

"Yep, that's the one. He was big on pool," said

DeMarco.

"Well thanks for your time and cooperation. If we need anything you'll be hearing from us," said detective Lane.

Mr. DeMarco quickly got up and shook each one of the Detective's hands.

"Not a problem, my doors are always open," he said.

"Boy, Jake was a good man, he was really trying to get his life together..."

A little later, Lane drove Fisher home in her 2001 Mercedes-Benz. Lost in his train of thought, he couldn't help but think on how much of a stranger he had been to his brother. Luke never gave him the second chance that he had truly deserved...

The next day at the 23rd precinct Detectives Fisher

and Lane were filing paperwork on the case and sorting out files when Matthews walked in.

"Anything new besides what we've learned?" he asked.

"Nope," replied Fisher.

"The pool hall is open from Wednesday through Saturday so tomorrow we're going to check it out," said Lane.

"Sounds good, but I was thinking we should go Thursday or Friday instead," said Matthews.

"Matthews, it's open tomorrow. The sooner we can get some answers and leads, the better," pressed Fisher.

"I understand kid but anyone involved with the crime or possible informants who knew Jake wouldn't show up at the place with his death being so sudden. They'd be scared out of their wits to even resurface there," Matthews said.

Detective Lane had then cut in, "Look, we're going there tomorrow and that's all there is to it. The first 96 hours are critical when assembling as much information and evidence to a crime as possible. You're a senior detective in the homicide department Frank, you know better than that." Matthews took out both hands deep from within his pocket and raised them to show peace.

"Alright, it was just a suggestion. I'll see you guys tomorrow.

Gordon gave me the day off to plan my moving affairs," he said. He then looked towards detective Lane and said, "I already told Fisher over here that once this case is solved I'm calling it quits.

I've given this job 30 years and I think it's time for

me to enjoy what's left of my life."

"We've got it under control over here, see you at

the pool hall tomorrow afternoon, 2p.m." said

Fisher.

Matthews nodded to express that he got the picture

and without another word, left.

The next day Fisher headed over to Jibbs alone. He

had agreed to meet up with Lane and Matthews

right in front of the establishment. As he waited for

them to arrive, Fisher lit up a cigarette.

After twenty minutes or so, Lane appeared, followed

by Matthews a couple of moments later. Together

they walked inside and as they passed between

aisles,

they saw people drinking beer and lining up pocket-

balls as they chatted and got into games.

The three detectives then approached a heavy set

man at the main counter.

"Can I help you?" he asked.

"Yeah, do you run this place," asked Fisher, as he

curiously looked around.

"Yeah, what is it you need?" he asked gruffly.

"BKPD," Lane said, as she hoisted her badge to

show the golden emblazoned shield.

In an instant the owner of the hall's demeanor

changed.

"How can I be of help officers?" he now asked

nervously.

"We're looking for three fellas who come here

sometimes; Smoke, Jeff, and Trey. Perhaps you may

know them?" questioned Fisher.

"Of course, they're regulars. They're here on most nights. In fact, they're right over there!" he said. As he pointed across the counter which separated himself from the cops, he pinpointed upon three young black men who appeared to be in their late twenties. They were all gathered at the pool table laughing in the midst of a game.

"Thanks, that will be all," said Lane. As casually as possible, the three detectives made their way to the table where the three men were playing. Once they had reached the table, the three men looked up.

"BKPD," said Matthews, as they all came to a halt.

"So, you guys happen to know Jake?" he asked. The three men suddenly dropped their pool sticks and stopped playing their game.

"Yeah, he's a cool guy," said one with the beer in his hand.

"Well he's dead, he died late last Saturday night by homicide; what do you guys know about that?" asked Fisher.

"Oh shit, Jake Fish?! Damn, he was worried about his safety too," said the same man with the beer.

"Who are you?" asked Lane.

"They call me Smoke but my real name is Bernard Robinson."

"You three mind going in for questioning downtown?" asked Fisher.

"No not at all, we were on good terms with Jake, anything we can do to help is fine," said the tallest of the bunch.

Back at the 23rd precinct, detective Fisher

interviewed Bernard, while Lane interviewed Jeff and

Matthews interviewed Trey.

"When was the last time you saw the victim?"

asked Fisher.

"Thursday night. He came in once he got off

work," said Robinson.

"Did you notice anything unusual? Anything at

all?"

"I remembered that he was confronted by three

men. Apparently he had done something wrong that

stemmed from his years of selling weight on the

street."

"What happened?" asked Fisher.

"There was a lot of pushing and shoving until

there was a separation. One of them even told him

to watch his back," Robinson said.

"You got any names for me?" asked Fisher.

"Ron Mercer, he usually wears a blue bandana, he's slim, well-built and wears an earring in his left ear," added Robinson.

"Where can I find him?" asked Fisher.

"I can't tell you that." He said.

"Why can't you?" asked Fisher in a vexed tone. Fisher who normally kept his cool was now losing his patience.

"I know nothing about him. I just know his name is big on the streets."

"Fine. You're free to go, if we need any more information, we'll be in contact."

Robinson quickly got up without another word and left.

Fisher sat in silence for about five minutes before he left the interrogation room. He hadn't slept well in days.

Every night that he went home, Jennifer was usually asleep.

And at six every morning he'd wake up to go back to the precinct to file more paperwork.

Once he was done with Robinson he decided to leave the office.

He then met Lane in the hallway walking towards him.

"What did you get?" she asked.

"Apparently there was an altercation last Thursday night with Jake and three men.

One of them with a blue bandana told him to watch his back after words," Fisher explained.

"That's the same exact information I got out of Jeff," replied Lane.

"Where's Matthews?" asked Fisher.

"He just got done interrogating Trey, he's on his way," she said.

Five minutes later, Matthews was seen turning the corner which led from his office.

"Wasn't there that night. Anything he said was redundant from our previous questionings of DeMarco and little Ms. Watson," he said.

"The only name and possible lead we have is this guy named Ron Mercer. Mercer...Mercer... I've heard that name before, why does it sound so familiar?" Fisher asked them curiously.

Both Lane and Matthews gave him muddled looks.

Then Lane suddenly said, "You know, that name

does sound vaguely familiar for some reason.

"So where do we go from here?" asked Fisher.

"It's getting late, why don't we pick this up tomorrow?" said Matthews, who seemed a bit perturbed.

They all mutually agreed and went their separate ways. That same night when Fisher got home, he spent all his time with Jennifer.

It was the first time in two weeks that they had spent quality time together since the heist case. As they sat on the couch and watched the New York Knicks and Boston Celtics basketball game, Fisher's cell phone started to beep.

Fisher pushed the talk button on his Nextel flip and said, "What's new cap?"

Captain Gordon in his deep resonant voice asked,

"Any leads?"

"Just some guy who happens to wear a blue bandana named Ron Mercer. Possible gang member I suppose. Apparently he knew Jake from back in the day. I'm guessing they had unfinished business," said Fisher.

"Now I'm giving you as long as you need for this case but just remember that Matthews will be retiring and moving within the next three months," said Gordon.

Fisher held the talk button for several seconds before he said,

"It's okay, I'll find out the person behind this with or without Matthews."

"I have the upmost faith in you Fisher, I'm not worried at all. Good night," he said.

"Night," Fisher responded.

A month passed by and it seemed as if the three detectives were riding upon a Ferris wheel.

People who knew Jake Fisher were in and out of the precinct like clockwork. Detectives Fisher, Lane, and Matthews ended up in dead ends and false leads everywhere that they turned. On many occasions detective Matthews told Fisher that he admired his grit and his intentions to seek justice but that the case was in dead water.

Even Lane was frustrated but didn't let her feelings surface.

Christmas had passed and with it came the news of a man being drowned in Coney Island. But that was a case for another squad and a different day.

The new year had arrived and with it came frigid

temperatures.

As January approached its end, each day passed with no news or info linked to the case.

Rumors swirled throughout the department on closing it.

But one day in particular, Lane happened to catch Fisher in his office.

"There's something extremely odd about our dilemma," she said. Fisher who had been skimming through the repetitive information that they had gathered over the last two months looked up at her.

"What do you mean by that?" he asked.

"Let me put it this way. Don't you think by now we should have found something?

It's almost like every time we learn something new, someone sweeps our footprints.

We've looked left and right and we haven't found

Ron Mercer. Why is that? And I'm pretty sure that

the both of us have heard his name before but I'm

not sure where.

These are the questions we've got to ask ourselves,"

she said exasperatedly.

Fisher nodded his head in complete agreement.

"Yes, it's definitely something I've been asking

myself. I recognized his name the moment Robinson

mentioned it to me," he admitted.

Valentine's day had now arrived and Fisher had just

gotten home with Jennifer. They had went to see the

opening of The Lion King on broadway and had

just came from eating dinner at Cher Maurice's in

Manhattan. Jennifer had long been in bed when

the clock struck 12 and the telephone suddenly

rang.

Fisher then proceeded to pick up.

"Hello?" he said.

"Fisher, its Gordon," said the captain.

At that precise moment Fisher suddenly shook any

inch of sleep that he may have had.

"Talk to me captain," he said.

"Detective Lane happened to find the two men

who were involved in the scuffle with your brother

back in mid-November. They were scared out of

their minds, and since Mercer was nowhere to be

found they assumed that they themselves could die

at the hands of murder at any time," said Gordon.

"Why is that?" asked Fisher.

"Well, remember that body that was found dead

on Coney Island two days after you, Lane, and

Matthews had gone to the pool hall?"

"Yeah, just after we had found out three possible suspects were involved."

"Well it turns out that the body happened to be that of Ron Mercer, the exact same guy that we were looking for," he said.

"So he was the true culprit then?" asked Fisher.

"Yes, but judging that he was forcefully drowned in Coney Island it seems as if he either had a beef or someone didn't want him found alive." said Gordon.

"It's funny how you mention that because once me, Lane and Matthews found him as a legit suspect, we couldn't find a trace of him.
It was as if he fell off the face of the earth," exclaimed Fisher.

"Exactly, and his two friends didn't want to end up

in his predicament so they've been hiding out in Long Island."

"Well thanks for the news cap. I'm going to inform Matthews and I'll speak to Lane tomorrow—"

"Fisher," Gordon cut in...

"Matthews is nowhere to be found...I haven't seen him in a week.

There's no sign of life at his house and he's seemed to have disappeared once Ron Mercer was found dead.

Remember when I had gave him the Ron Mercer case during the whole crossfires at 59th debacle?"

He then continued, "Detective Lane had just remembered that she had heard the name inside her office of the burglary squad room."

After what seemed like an eternal moment, Fisher

almost dropped the receiver when he heard Gordon's answer...Could he really believe what he had just heard? He felt pangs of anger boil inside of him...Thoughts began to swirl in his head as if he were trapped within a tornado...The whole time Matthews worked beside him...The whole time they seemed completely baffled as to the whereabouts of Jake's killer...Yes, Ron Mercer wanted Jake dead but he paid someone to commit the crime...Now he remembered where he had heard the name. When the 59th and Columbus case was under investigation, Matthews had one day appeared in Lane's office and was given the Ron Mercer case. How could he have been so stupid? When Jake went to prison in 93', he had ratted on a kid named Chauncey Matthews who was a fellow dealer to the weight that Jake was selling on the streets.

Chauncey had went to prison and had died by inmate brutality. Detective Matthews had been bitter that his nephew had gotten murdered. Matthews never had kids of his own and had treated Chauncey like a son. They were always seen together before 93'.

Anyone within the BKPD had known the story, Chauncey had truly been detective Matthews's pride and joy...

Matthews had even interrogated Luke himself when he was just 22 and was trying to turn his life around. There was a murder at the time on a kid named Evan Wright. He was a drug dealer that worked hand in hand with Jake as well. Fisher should've thought of this the day Matthews had decided to take the assignment.

In the mind of Frank Matthews there had never been a case...

The conclusion to the crime had always been misguided...

There was nothing else that Fisher could do...

Matthews had talked months before about calling it quits once the case was over...

And now...

It really was over...

Fisher had to accept the fact that unless granted a miracle, he knew it was done...

Jake had been his blood brother but he died to Luke Fisher a stranger and as for Frank Matthews the homicide detective himself, he'd make sure to never be heard from again.

Misguided indeed...

Case closed.

Part III: "FRANKLY TWISTED"

As Told by Detective Frank Matthews

Intro

Let me make this clear. Quite frankly, I've been a twisted individual for as long as I can remember. I think it all goes back to when my mother dropped me on my head as a baby; but that bit of information is irrelevant. Anyway, where are my manners? Allow me to introduce myself...I go by the name of Matt Frank, formerly known as Detective Frank Matthews of Parkside Brooklyn's, 23rd precinct. I'm currently located on a tropical island sipping a well-stirred margarita just 24 hours removed from Valentine's day. I can't tell you exactly where, because if I did, I'd simply have to kill you. The sun is currently out and shining while cops in New York are left with the task of cleaning up my bloody mess. How long will it take for Fisher to figure it out? Here's my response: Doesn't matter. It's no longer my problem that's for sure. His brother brought it upon himself. I'll soon turn 66 this spring and I need to enjoy every precious minute on earth before I eternally rot in hell. But just remember that behind every movement, there is a reason for madness...So now, before I bring you up to speed...let me take you back to where it all started. About 10 years ago, 1993...

It was a Friday night, February 16th, and I had just pulled up to my usual spot.

After a long hard day of work I always went to the Trash Bar.

"Frankie," said the bartender as I walked in.

"Timmy," I replied, as I took a seat at the bar.

"What will it be?" he asked in a fond tone.

"Give me a Long Island iced tea and please don't

water it down," I told him.

"Anything for you Frank," he said, as he delivered my drink.

"What's been going on my man?" I asked, as I surveyed the scene.

"Nothing much Frankie. I've just been having problems getting it up with Stace," he said as he put a fist under his chin and leaned upon the bar's counter.

"A little bit of drugs will help you hold it up," I told him.

"Awww it's nothin," he replied, as he wiped an empty glass. He then continued, "That's the price I get for going out with a 26 year old house realtor. I guess she likes the sugar I'm holding. And you know what they say Frankie, the blacker the berry—"

"The sweeter the juice," I replied, as I finished the content of my drink.

"You're a fool Timmy."

We then erupted with laughter.

In the midst of our laughter, my pager started to go off.

"Awww shit, what could this man possibly want at 3 in the morning?" I whined.

"Oh boy, another case?" asked Tim as he took the empty glass and stared at my pager.

"Yeah, where's your phone Tim? I gotta call that son-of-a-bitch Gordon."

"It's right down the hall. Just bust a left once you reach the men's restroom."

"Thanks," I said.

As I reached the phone, I quickly returned Gordon's

call from the 23rd precinct.

"Hello?" said a man in a brisk tone.

"Good morning, how may I be of help at this hour?" I replied stiffly.

"Matthews, there's been a murder at the Bedford-Stuyvesant housing projects. At 2 a.m. this morning a drug dealer by the name of Evan Wright was killed. My guess is that the drug pushers within the area had something to do with it."

"Give me the address," I told him.

"1120 and Bedford Avenue," he said.

"Ok, I'll be there first thing in the morning," I replied.

"Detective Alvin Alvin has already been informed and he'll meet you there as well."

"How many times do I have to tell you Gordon, I

don't need no damn partner!"

"Detective Alvin Alvin is one of our best and you two have been working well together in the past 5 years so don't give me this bull---"

"That's because you've got the kid following me around like paparazzi and---"

"Enough!" yelled Captain Gordon.

"I'm tired of you always complaining about the kid. He does great work and as long as you're under my watch you're stuck with him understand?"

"Do you understand?" commanded Gordon in a voice of authority.

"Yes," I said with contempt.

"Good."

"See you tomorrow," I said in resent.

"Bye," he replied coldly.

Filling you in: As I hung up the phone, I couldn't help but think how much I hated Captain James Gordon. We had both gotten into the 23rd precinct at the age of 25 and by the time we were both 40, the police commissioner decided to make him Captain within our precinct instead of me. The result of that was a deteriorated once close friendship. I mean, the man is my age for Christ's sake. So why the hell should I call him Captain? There is never a day that I call him that. And so, as I put the phone back onto its wall-jack behind the counter, I said a quick goodbye to Tim as I went out the door...

The next day I pulled up to the spot of the crime scene in my 1982 Honda Accord. "So what if I drive a shitty car? You can't expect to live the lavish life when you've got Gordon calling the shots. I swear on my life that the position he holds should be mine...In that precise moment, detective Alvin pulled up behind me in his new 1992 Lexus. As he exited his car I noticed he was wearing an ocean blue trench coat, suede shoes, Calvin Klein jeans and black Fendi sunglasses as he approached me. He was a very good looking black man at the age of 32."

"How are you Frank?" he asked, as he locked his car door.

"I'm okay and you?" I asked.

I don't care: To be honest, I really didn't give six shits on how he felt.

"I'm alright," he replied. "I think Captain Gordon is waiting for us by the building."

"Yeah, he is," I replied uninterestedly.

"Let's go see what we've got," he said.

As we approached the front door of the project building, Gordon greeted us and led us to a side alley of the housing unit.

"What do we got here?" I asked, as me and Alvin

made our way past the do-not-cross yellow crime scene tape.

"Evan Wright," said coroner Murray as the forensic photographer took pictures of the corpse. He then continued, "A 20 year old drug dealer, shot three times in the head. Possible 9 millimeter bullet wounds and literally broken in two from the hip down."

"Where is he?" asked detective Alvin as he cringed at the coroner's description.

"In there," said Gordon reluctantly as he pointed towards the dumpster.

Alvin and I then proceeded towards the dumpster. The sight wasn't pretty.

Wright was literally broken in half so that his torso was disconnected from the lower region of his body.

The lifeless Wright was also left naked with three gunshot wounds to the forehead giving him the resemblance of a human bowling ball.

Alvin finally ripped his eyes off the disturbing sight when he managed to ask, "Any ideas on who could have done this?"

"No, not really but whoever did it wanted him worse than dead. Our guess is that they used a machete to cleanly saw him in half," said coroner Murray as he began to extract body samples with blood and placed them within a forensic plastic bag.

Realization: It had just only hit me on who the kid happened to be. Evan used to be a drug runner for Ron Mercer, the kingpin of BedStuy's drug trafficking. It left me amazed as to what the kid could have done to have ended up in such a terrible state. Also, my nephew Chauncey worked for this

Mercer. I had to get to the bottom of it as quickly as I could...

"Matthews! Alvin! You both are to report as quickly as you can to the precinct in order to get an investigation of suspects underway. By Monday, I want you guys out there in as many places as possible to see if you can resolve the matter," said Gordon.

"Sure thing cap," said Alvin.

"You got it," I said as we left the gruesome crime scene and headed towards our cars.

"I'll meet you back at the precinct Frank," said Alvin.

"I'm going home first," I replied.

"But Frank, it's not even noon yet. This isn't the time for a break," said Alvin sternly.

I had then stopped dead in my tracks to set him

straight. Once I turned around, I let him have it.

"First off, watch your tone when talking to me

boy," I said calmly.

"Secondly, I'm old enough to be your father so

don't tell me what I can and can't do.

"Thirdly, I don't like you. I never have, and I never

will. I just hate everything about you from your well-

liked personality, your G.Q. appearance and that

stupid name your mother gave you.

"Honestly, who names their kid after their own last

name. Alvin Alvin? Really? So don't question me boy.

I'm going home and I'll meet you at the precinct

within an hour, got it?"

"Got it," said Alvin as he quickly went to his car.

Case Solved: As I watched him pull off I had to go see Chauncey. By no means did I want him involved in this murder rap. And so, as quickly as I had gotten into my car, I proceeded to make my way to East 21st between Rogers Avenue and Cortelyou Road. When I arrived at 21st and Rogers, I quickly made my way to apartment 4D.

As I knocked on the door someone said,

"Who is it?"

"It's me, Big Matthews!" I answered.

"Big Matthews, what's up man?" said the guy who opened the door.

"Nothing much, can I come in?" I asked.

"Yeah, sure," he said as he shut the door behind me.

"Where's Lil' Matt?" I asked.

"Oh, he just stepped out to get something for Ron. He'll be back."

"Where's Mercer?" I then asked.

"He's in the back."

And as I made my way into a dark room, I saw Mercer who was all alone counting money to his own pleasure.

"Ayyy," he said as I shook his hand.

Ron was a stubby black man who stood about 5'6, had bad wrinkles across his forehead and looked as if he had sniffed white for years. His eye bags gave hints that he had been sleep deprived for days. To top it all, he was gang affiliated. Ron always wore a blue bandana forever showing his loyalty and allegiance to the crips.

"How can I be of service to you Big Matt?" he asked.

"Where's Chauncey?" I asked.

"He should be here any minute," said Mercer.

"I sent him to collect some money of mine on Beverley and Nostrand."

As Ron Mercer finished telling me this, it was then that his doorbell rang.

"In fact, I think that's him now, Jake go check the door."

As quickly as he could, Jake ran to the hallway and soon returned with Chauncey.

Chauncey happened to be the son of my deceased little brother Lucas Matthews. He was a mischievous kid who I could always remember getting in trouble even on his days at the playground. He stood about 6'1, was brown skinned, hard-faced and wore a high afro that could've put him in the 70's. He also had a few strands under his chin that I always poked fun of to go along with his affinity for toothpicks.

"What brings you here unc?" he asked as I embraced him in a hug.

"I wanted to have a talk with you three," I said.

"I've got some time, I'll finish counting the rest of this loot later," said Mercer as he stuffed the cheese into an old shabby drawer.

"What's on your mind?" he asked.

"Evan's dead," I told him as I waited in a long dreary silence.

"So?" he asked when he eventually spoke.

"Why is that?" I asked patiently.

"Because he deserved it!" he yelled as he banged his fist upon the wobbly wooden table that he leaned against.

"Calm down," I said as I proceeded to sit in an

old and feeble chair.

"The kid was asking for it Big Matt. I gave him 20 grand to hold and he decided to trade all of my loot for a coke deal uptown!"

"BX?" I asked curiously.

"Yeah, and when I pressed him about it, he told me that he simply wanted out and that he was expanding his business ventures."

"Sounds like the son-of-a-bitch got what he deserved then," I said as I twiddled my thumbs.

"Exactly! The nerve of him to wanna expand upon his so-called business ventures. How foolish does that sound? I've been hustlin' since that kid was in diapers Matt. I'm talkin' bout early 70's, afro-sheen, big comb, tooth-pick–and-all watching Shaft. I mean, Michael Jackson was bad but he wasn't even off the wall at the time! Now all of a sudden,

some kid who doesn't even have hair on his nuts

wants to be a boss?" asked Mercer rhetorically, as he

extracted his money out of the old feeble

drawer and resumed counting.

"Shit, you just gotta watch yourself out here

Mercer. Thanks to you there's a whole lotta heat I

gotta cover up back at the department."

"I'm sorry about that Big Matt. I didn't mean for it

to be that way."

"Just say you'll lay low for a while. I've gotta find

someone to put this wrap on."

"Will do," he said as he began to smoke a blunt.

"Well I'm already late, let me get started on this

case," I said as I got up.

"Chauncey, shut the door behind your uncle," said

Mercer.

"It's ok Ron. Chauncey, walk me outside son," I said as I got up to leave the apartment.

When we reached my car, Chauncey noticed that I had a lot on my mind and asked,

"Everything good unc?"

"Yeah, but you know this is a lot of shit for me to cover back at the office. Now promise me you'll stay out of trouble in the meantime."

"Yeah, I will," he obliged.

"And another thing. Only trust yourself. Don't put all of your faith in Jake and Mercer...You know...you should be leaving this kind of life behind. Go back to school..."

"School's not for me," he said as he watched an ambulance wail its way through a red light.

He then turned back around to face me. After a few moments of intense gaze he then said, "This is my life."

From where I stood with one hand perched on the roof of my Honda, I began to heave a huge sigh.

"Ok, but just know that eventually the game always ones up the score in the end.

And watch your back with Mercer, if he can do what he did to Evan, he won't hesitate to do it to you."

I then continued, "I won't think twice about killing him if I have to. Quite frankly, I've never liked the cumstain."

Chauncey let out a huge burst of laughter.

"I'm serious. Just look out for yourself kiddo," I said in a sort of pleading way.

"I will unc," he said.

I do care: After giving him a quick one armed hug and kiss to the forehead, I quickly got into my car and went as fast as I could to the 23rd precinct. I didn't want Gordon to notice my long peculiar absence after he had placed me on such an important case. But it wasn't the first time Gordon gave orders and I didn't respond. I often did that on the regular...

As soon as I reached the station I quickly went into my office where I found Detective Alvin stationed on my computer. He wasn't wasting any time as a donut was seen crammed into his mouth as he quickly gathered a list of suspects.

"Find anything yet?" I asked.

"I've found a list of names that we can quickly start interrogating but that's about it. And you?"

"Jeez, I just got here kid. Can I at least take a moment to breathe first?"

"Sorry, and by the way Gordon wants to talk to us but he wants you to go get him. I think he's in the burglary unit."

"Whatever," I said, as I left the room.

"Just like Gordon," I thought.

"Always wants to talk but you always gotta be the one to find him. I knew exactly where he was though. Gordon was often found in detective Deborah Lane's office up in the burglary unit on the east wing."

When I opened the door, Gordon looked up at me and said,

"Oh, you're here. Did you finally get a list of suspects?"

"Yeah, the kid and I found a list of four names to look into," I said.

"Great," he said as he made advancements to where I stood by the door.

He then turned around and told the female sitting at the desk,

"Lane, I'll be back."

Clarification: The reason Gordon was always in the burglary department was because he had deep feelings for this new girl by the name of detective Deborah Lane. Although she was much younger than both of us, she was very mature and insightful for her age. And as we left, I couldn't help but think on what a cute thing she actually was. She was 24, with no man, and no kids. And if I had the chance, I would've gave it to her good the only way I knew how...Women often told me that I was as long as a ruler and as wide as a remote. Shame on you, if you don't understand what I'm currently bringing to your attention...

As we got back into the office, Gordon pulled up a chair besides detective Alvin and asked,

"Okay, so what do we have?"

"There are four possible names that come up with Evan Wright," said Alvin. He then continued, "They all happen to have known him nonetheless."

"Give me some names," demanded Gordon.

"Well, the first name on the list is Violetta Wright, the kid's grandmother. Word going around is that she was the last person to see him alive," said Alvin.

"We've also got a Ray Chandler," I said.

"Who's he?" asked Gordon.

"Former friend of our victim, maybe he has the scoop on why things happened the way they did."

In that precise moment, Detective Alvin Alvin gave me a look of suspicion. The name had not appeared on his list of suspects and judging by the look he gave me, he was obviously wondering where on earth I had found such precise information. But just remember, Wright used to run with my nephew along with the likes of Ron Mercer. So I definitely ran a background check on who ever that he came into contact with...

"Any others?" asked Gordon.

"There's a Chris Palmer, a bouncer at the Palladium Nightclub in the city that Wright used to attend. They once got into a verbal altercation, and word going around is that they never liked each other," said Alvin.

"Sounds good, so let's see if we can get st—"

"I forgot to mention, there's a Luke Fisher as well. A former drug dealer now gone straight. He currently resides on East 93rd in Canarsie," added Alvin, as he looked over his police report.

2 Fishers, 1 Truth: My heart suddenly gave a jolt like some jumping cables. Fisher? Could he be related to Jake Fisher by any chance perhaps? If Fisher did have a brother, how come he hadn't told me? If they were related by any chance, this would surely put Chauncey at risk of being in trouble. I had to find out as soon as possible whether the two were related or not...

"So where's your first destination," asked Gordon in his usual brisk tone.

"Grandma's house of course. Most likely she can set up the whole trail as we go along," assured Alvin.

"Okay, get to it. Keep me posted as you guys go along," said Gordon.

"We will," I said as all three of us made movements to leave the room.

Once Gordon had went back down towards the east wing and I was sure he was out of earshot, I calmly asked Alvin,

"Where'd you get the info on Fisher?"

"He was a drug dealer not too long ago," replied

Alvin. He then continued,

"I've got a few connects in the streets and they

told me about him. To be honest, I don't think he's

really that important, I just thought he'd be another

name to round out our list of suspects, but why is

that important?" he asked as he eyed me

suspiciously.

"No reason," I replied casually.

"And what about this Chandler hmm?" he added.

"Last time I checked, you weren't here when I was

doing all the work."

"That's why I went home kid. I do all of my damn

homework on my own time. That's how I operate," I

said.

As we approached the parking lot where our cars stood one in front of the other, Detective Alvin made a move towards my car.

"How many times do I have to tell you Alvin, I work alone and quite frankly if the decisions were strictly mine, I wouldn't need a damn partner!"

Detective Alvin then shifted his walk north to where his car stood at the end of the lot.

Shady rule #1: (*Work Alone*) If you have someone around you constantly, nine times out of ten they are going to know a lot about you and how you work. And personally, I felt that as a two-way detective, I didn't need that. The last thing I wanted was a fellow detective on my ass keeping up with everything I did...

Half an hour later, we pulled up separately at Violetta Wright's door. She lived on East 29th and

Beverly Road. I then proceeded to ring the doorbell as we waited for a response.

"Who is it?" she asked in a weak voice.

"BKPD," I said.

As quickly as I had said it, the door opened. Mrs. Wright had on a cooking apron with gloves and mittens as she held a very big spoon. Her hair was placed in rollers and a house net as she prepped for a meal or whatever it was that she had been conjuring in the kitchen.

"Come on in," she said.

As we entered the home which smelled like vegetable soup and vicks vapor rub, the old woman then pointed towards her dingy old couch.

"Sit down," she said.

"That's okay. We'd like to make this brief while

asking you a few questions Madam," I said, as I was in no mood to get comfortable.

"I'm guessing this is about my grandson. Well, let me tell you something, I loved Evan with all my heart but he got what was coming to him. Do you know how many times I told that boy what would happen if he kept going at the rate he did? I was left to raise him. I had him since he was five years old." In that moment, Mrs. Wright decided to sit down. She was a very old woman indeed and it was obvious that her excitement had gotten the best of her.

"Are you alright M'am?" asked Alvin.

"I'm okay," she replied as she twiddled her thumbs upon the big spoon at hand.

"What happened to his parents?" I asked.

"The same exact thing. His father, was my son but

he and his girlfriend, Evan's mother, were shot to death while trying to fight a rival drug gang back in 1978."

"Wow," said Alvin in disbelief.

"I know, I know, now he's ended up like his parents. I've had high blood pressure for the past 20 years, and so, I was never able to deal with him. I always knew that he would end up the way they did.

"Anything else we should know about your grandson?" I said.

"He used to be very good friends with this kid named Ray. A very nice young boy who is currently in school trying to make something out of himself...If only Evan could have been more like him," said the old woman as she sighed.

"Is the kid's full name Ray Chandler by any

chance?" asked Alvin as he wrote notes into a little

notepad that he had suddenly pulled out.

"Yes, he's the one," said Mrs. Wright as she stared

out of her cloudy window.

"That will be all," I said.

"Thanks again M'am and if anything comes up we

will be in touch," said Alvin as we both made our

way towards the door.

"Not a problem, I'm glad that I could be of help,"

she said before shutting the door behind us.

After leaving the porch of Mrs. Wright, Detective

Alvin then asked me,

"Where can we find this kid?"

"NYU," I replied. "He's a sophomore there and

lives on campus."

"Let me guess, you found that out during your

personal homework session?"

asked Alvin as we both reached our cars.

"Now you're starting to get me kid," I chuckled as I

opened my car door.

"Three hours of work left, what now?" asked Alvin.

"C'mon, it's a Saturday and the kid's a college

student, he's probably planning on going out

tonight. I say we pay him a visit ASAP to see what

we can squeeze out of him before then," I said.

"You got it," replied Alvin as he fired up his engine

and left without another word.

Shady rule #2: (*Know the personnel*): I soon left a
minute after Alvin as I headed to New York
University. And as for me knowing the boy's school
of attendance, that's easy. Mercer knew even the
most personal details of all his employees. It was the
most secure way to keeping himself safe. But in
terms of myself just knowing that piece of

information in general, there's one thing you've got to remember; I'm Detective Frank Matthews...I know everything...

An hour later, after very bad traffic, I arrived at New York University located on 383 Lafayette Street. About five minutes or so after I had got there, I noticed detective Alvin had parked his car parallel to where I had been on the opposite side of the street. As he got out of his car and made his way to where I had been standing on the curb he asked,

"Do you know which residency hall that he lives in?"

"No, but let's go check out administration, they'll tell us," I said.

"Shit, there are probably at least a dozen of residency buildings in this damn place," said Alvin as he took in the sights of the large beautiful campus.

"That's why I'm not going to waste my damn time

searching for one measly kid,"

I replied in a matter of fact tone.

As we entered the Students Services Center, both

Alvin and I made our way towards a female

receptionist who was sitting behind a glass window.

"You talk to her kid, you're much more of a people

person than I am," I said, as I sat down in a waiting

chair.

"Excuse me miss," said Alvin as he approached the

woman.

"Yes?" she quickly replied as she took in Alvin's

dashing good looks.

"I'm with the BKPD on official business," he said

as he flashed his badge.

"Can you tell me in which residency hall I'll find Ray Chandler?"

"One minute please," she said as she typed his name on the computer in front of her.

"Yes, Raymond is in Thirteenth Street Hall. Just walk right back out of these doors, walk up one block to East 13th Street and you can't miss it."

"Thanks again," he said kindly as he flashed his charming smile.

We then proceeded to exit the building.

"You're better than me kid. I dislike people. Better yet, I hate them. If there's no need for me to talk to them, I just won't," I said.

"Sometimes, I just don't know what to think about you Matthews," said Alvin as he shook his head in disbelief.

When we entered Thirteenth Street Hall, an R.A. told us that Chandler could be found on the third floor in room 3C.

As we made our way towards his room, Alvin began to knock on the door.

Loud music and commotion could be heard blaring from just within the door's exterior.

After what seemed like thirty seconds the door finally opened.

"Finally, we've been waiting for hours! Where's the pizza?" said the kid stupidly as he held the doorknob.

"Do I look like a delivery boy to you? I'm with the BKPD," I said as I flashed him my badge.

"Listen, I didn't do anything, I didn't mean to offend," said the kid in a stammer.

"A guilty conscious eh? What's your name kid?"
I asked him as I cracked a sly grin.

"Eric Bennett," he replied in fear.

"Look, you have to excuse my partner here, my
name is detective Alvin Alvin and we're looking for
your roommate Ray Chandler," said Alvin as we then
stepped into the room.

"Ray stepped out to do laundry about an hour
ago; he should be back any minute," said Eric,
unsure if he had heard Detective Alvin's name
correctly.

It was then that Ray Chandler walked in, laundry
sack and all. He was a pretty tall kid who stood
about 6'3", broad shouldered and had a very queasy
look about him. He was brown complexioned and
although he was tall and broad shouldered, it was

still obvious that he was just a kid no more than 19

or 20 years of age.

"Did the pizza get here?" he asked a he took in

the presence of Alvin and I.

"The pizza's here alright. And it's hot. BKPD," I

said as I now flashed him my badge.

"What's going on?" he asked nervously as he put

the clean sack of laundry on his bronze colored bed.

"Mr. Chandler, what do you know about the death

of Evan Wright?" asked Alvin sharply.

"Awww shit," he said as he closed his eyes and

shook his head.

"Well?" I asked.

"It's news to me. I mean, I wouldn't say I'm

completely shocked, but this is the first time I'm

hearing about it," he said as he now moved aside his

sack in order to sit upon the bed.

"When was the last time you saw him?" asked Alvin as he took out his notepad once again.

"During winter break. He stopped by my house on Franklin Avenue in Brooklyn just a little after Christmas."

"Is it safe to say that you two were the best of friends?" I asked.

"No—well—yes—I mean, we used to be but ever since sophomore year of High School we haven't really clicked. Evan became heavily involved with street life and I've never been one to indulge into that kind of trouble," he gushed.

"Do you know what could have placed him upon that path?" asked Alvin as he continued to scribble down notes at a frantic pace.

"Yeah, I remember him getting involved with a Luke Fisher back in 89' and ever since then he took a turn for the worst. But if everything you said is true, my guess is that the kid Luke is long gone as well."

"Not quite, he's living in Canarsie and we're definitely going to check him out," said Alvin, as he began to wrap up his notes.

"That will be all," I said. "If there's anything more that we need, we'll be in touch, but overall thanks for your help."

"No, thank you. I know Evan really got caught up but he was a good person with an even better heart," said Ray.

"Well, once again, thank you gentlemen for your time," said Alvin as we exited the room.

"Ok, next on the list is Mr. Palmer, but after

receiving that bit of info from the kid, I say we go straight to Fisher," said Alvin.

"No, let's see what this Palmer guy has to say. I have seniority over you Alvin, listen to what I'm telling you," I said.

"Okay, so I guess we'll check out the club tomorrow night?" he asked.

"Sounds like a plan," I replied.

And without another word, we both got into our cars and pulled off.

As I drove back to my apartment in Brownsville, I couldn't wait to phone Jake Fisher.

I just had to find out if that guy Luke was related to him or not.

The first thing I did was pour myself a drink of scotch once I had reached home.

After waking up from dozing off to a previous

taping of Saturday Night Live, it had just occurred to

me that I hadn't phoned Fisher.

I then proceeded to call Chauncey who then gave

me Fisher's number. After what seemed like seven

rings a voice finally answered.

"Hello?"

"Fisher is that you?" I said.

"Who is this?" he replied sleepily.

"Big Matt."

"Oh—hey what's up?" he asked still in a dream

like state.

"Now Fisher, be very careful with me because I'm

a dangerous man," I said.

"Why? Is everything ok?" he asked nervously.

"I'm only going to ask you this once, so I expect

you to tell me the truth."

"Yes, okay," he said more alert and awake than before.

"Are you by any chance related to a Luke Fisher?"

Silence ensued as I waited for him to respond.

"FISHER! Answer me!!!" I bellowed.

"No! C'mon man, even if I were, don't you think Mercer would know?" he tried to assure me.

"You know I don't like to waste my breath and so I pray that you're telling the truth," I said menacingly.

"I—I—I am," he said reluctantly.

"Okay, that's all I need to know. I'm sorry I woke you, get some rest," I said more relaxed now.

"Okay, will do, thanks," he said before hanging

up quickly. I then proceeded to take another sip of my scotch before my phone rang.

"Hello?" I said.

"Matthews, it's me Gordon."

"Damn it!" I thought.

Even in my own damn apartment I couldn't get away from that fruitcake...

"Yes," I responded, in the best polite voice I could possibly muster.

"How did the first day of investigation go?" he asked.

"It went smooth. We interrogated the kid's grandmother and then a former close friend of his not too long after that. We plan on investigating Palmer on Monday."

"What about the Fisher guy?" asked Gordon.

"We haven't gotten around to him as of yet but we'll try," I said.

"No, don't try Matthews. Do!" He then continued,

"This is a very lethal case. I mean the kid was literally cut in half here."

"I know, I'll be sure that we see to it; Guaranteed," I assured him.

"Good, I'll see you at work this upcoming week," he said.

"Sure thing," I said before I quickly hung up the phone.

If there was anyone who annoyed me the most it had to be Captain America of the 23rd precinct...

Two nights later, detective Alvin pulled up behind me at the Palladium Nightclub on East 14th between Irving Plaza and 3rd Avenue in Manhattan.

As we met on the sidewalk he asked,

"Do you know what this Chris Palmer guy looks like?"

"My guess is that he's the big black guy right over there by the door," I said as we skipped a line of people waiting to get into the club.

"Can I help you?" he asked as we made our way to the front.

As I took in his appearance I noticed that he was built as thick and tall as any NFL linebacker that I had ever seen. He stood about 6'4", dressed in all black, (as those bouncers usually do) was bald-headed and had a hoop earring in his left ear.

"Yes, BKPD," said Alvin. "We'd like to ask you a few questions if that's okay with you."

"Does it look like I answer questions?" He then

continued,

"I mean, you see me working here right? I've got a full line of customers waiting to get into this club tonight and here you guys come messing up the flow."

"First off all, these shitheads can wait," I said.

"Secondly, watch your tone Tommy from Martin. The man here asked if we could just pick your brain for a sec. I know you're happy that you finally got a job."

"What do you guys want?" he asked.

It was obvious that he was getting irritated.

"Do you know anything about the death of an Evan Wright?" asked Alvin.

"No, I don't. Heard about it though. The shit's been all over prime-time news.

He used to come here from time to time but it's been a year since I last seen him," said Palmer.

"Do you know any of the people he used to possibly run wi—?" started Alvin.

"Listen, get out of here! The both of you! If you want to ask questions, wait until I get off of work. If not, go speak to the manager in the back. Leave me be."

"Boy, if it wasn't for me being a cop, I would beat the hell out of you right now," I said as grim and candid as possible.

"Ha! You?" he laughed and then said,

"Old man, move it along, you're probably in your mid 50's, shouldn't you be back at the station telling these young bloods what to do while eating a glazed donut or somethin'?"

"Kid, you have no clue what you've gotten yourself into. I'll come back, sooner than later and when I do, I'm going to make you hurt boy."

"Right, but if you guys will excuse yourselves, I need to get back to what I was doing. And take Lawrence Fishburne with you," he said as he pointed at Alvin with a smirk.

"Let's just go," said Alvin as he tugged on my arm. As we walked away I couldn't help but think how much I wanted to hurt him.

"Next and last on our list is Luke Fisher. I say we go check him out tomorrow," Alvin said.

"I can't. Tomorrow's my day off. Let's check him out Thursday instead.
On Wednesday, I've got a shit load of paperwork to fill out," I told him.

"Agreed, I've got my own paperwork to take care of tomorrow as well. I'll see you Thursday then," he said, just before his Lexus pulled off into the night.

"FRANKLY TWISTED": Now, the following day I indeed had a day off. However, I decided to return to work at night...

I pulled up in front of the Palladium Nightclub at approximately 2 a.m. as I waited for Mr. Palmer to exit the premises.

About 15 minutes later, Palmer came out and locked up as he approached his 4x4 Ford pick-up truck. I was dressed in black attire with a hooded mask and navy blue Nike Air-Maxes when I crept up behind him. As he scrambled within his pockets for his car keys I tapped him slightly on the shoulder. When he turned around, I punched him so hard in the face

that his top almost spun off like a dreidel. And as he
lied on the floor out cold I then whispered:
"Who's the old man now Tommy? You know, before
you mess with the big leaguers, make sure you
master the minors."

And with no hesitancy I bent his left elbow back
until I heard a snap. His gold earring was shining
upon the night's sky before I wrapped my fingers
around its hoop and yanked it out of his ear,
splitting his lower earlobe in two. I threw what
was now a bloody earring on his chest as I left him
sprawled out upon the frigid ground...

On Thursday afternoon, I parked my car just behind
Alvin's Lexus, just near Fisher's Canarsie apartment.
As I met him, I asked whether he knew which
apartment we were heading into.

"5E," he said as we made our way into the building.

"Cool," I replied.

We had then stepped into the main entrance elevator as it would take us to the fifth floor.

"Hey, did you hear?" asked Alvin.

"What is it?" I asked as I began to chew my tongue.

"Palladium security guard Chris Palmer was found unconscious in front of the establishment. Someone split open his earlobe and broke his left elbow."

"Oh Yeah? Well would you look at that? I knew that son—of—a—bitch had something coming to him. He's lucky that it wasn't me. I would've done worse," I said.

"Yeah, he sure is," chuckled Alvin with two hands

deep within his trench coat pockets.

When we reached the fifth floor and found 5E, I proceeded to wrap my knuckles upon the door.

A few moments later when the door opened, a young man of about 22 years of age stood before me.

2 Fishers, 1 lied: In that moment I almost lost it. There was no doubt in my mind that this kid was related to Jake.

"BKPD," said Alvin.

"Come on in," said Luke.

He stood about 6'1", had a very athletic appearance and seemed laid back.

"We'd like to know if you knew anything surrounding the parameters of Evan Wright's death," said Alvin.

"No sir, I have no clue. It's been three years since I last saw or spoke to him."

"And how did you know him?" asked Alvin.

"I used to be a drug dealer myself in BedStuy's Marcy Projects." He then continued,

"All of that's behind me now. I almost died at gunpoint for a coke deal which went bad. That's when I realized that the street life wasn't my calling."

"But how did you meet him?" I interjected.

"I met him through my brother who wanted me to show him the ropes on how the game worked."

"What's your brother's name?" asked Alvin.

"Nice try but I'm not telling you that," said Luke as he sat down upon a battered chair.

"Mr. Fisher, you do know that you're withholding information from the BKPD that can punish you for up to ten years in federal prison," said Alvin.

"Look, I haven't even seen my brother in four years. Who knows where he is.

As far as I know, he's dead to me."

"Well then, thanks for your time," said Alvin.

"But just remember if nothing comes up, we will be back for you," he added.

"Listen, I plan on taking that police exam in a few weeks okay. I've been studying law for quite some time now. I think I know my rights," said Fisher.

"Thank you Fisher, let's go Alvin," I said.

"What the hell is wrong with you Matthews?" said Alvin, once we were headed down the elevator.

"You barely spoke in there," he added.

"Sometimes, it's best to just stay quiet, and besides, you were doing pretty well on your own. I figured you had it all under control," I told him as I tried to manage my nerves.

"Yeah, I guess. Look, we need to find this other Fisher guy, and fast. I think once we find him all the pieces will begin to fit accordingly," said Alvin.

"Listen, I'm going home, I've got some things to take care of, tell Gordon that I'll be down at the station real soon."

"Sure thing," said Alvin as he left without another word.

As I got into my car and watched him pull off, all I could think about was how Fisher lied and denied having a brother. He played me for a sucker. There was just no way I would let Chauncey get hurt by any means.

Later that day, I phoned up the 23rd precinct and

told them Jake Fisher's location.

The following night he was arrested. Caught in possession with 90 grams of cocaine and had been sentenced to 15 years in prison. For me, it was a great way to personally end the case.

 To avoid any suspicions I constantly ducked and dodged all interrogations that would consist of me and Fisher being in the same vicinity. And so, I personally thought that Jake's arrest was the end all be all. But man was I wrong...

Two weeks later I made my usual Friday night appearance at the Trash Bar when a seat by the counter suddenly became available.

 "Hey, look who it is?" said Tim as I settled in.

 "Just give me the hardest liquor of whatever you

have," I said as I looked around.

"Tough case?" asked Tim curiously.

"No, not really," I said, "I knew where it was going from the start."

"I see," he said as he pondered upon what I meant.

He then poured the content and handed me the concoction of my drink.

Before I was given the chance to consume it, my pager suddenly went off.

"Geez, it's almost midnight," I said as I looked at the number in annoyance.

"Does Gordon's wife give him any amount of ass?" I added.

Tim suddenly burst into laughter.

"I need to use your phone Timmy."

"You know where it's at," he replied.

As I made my way towards the phone and dialed Gordon's number, it wasn't long before he quickly answered.

"Matthews," he said.

"Gordon," I replied.

"Listen, we were trying to work out a plea deal for Fisher to reduce his sentence and apparently he gave us a name in which I'm not sure rings a bell to you."

"Yes?" I said as waited with bated breath.

"Chauncey Matthews," he said.

In that moment everything seemed surreal. I dropped the receiver to the floor and lost my oxygen in a way that I hadn't the 55 years prior...

I had worked so hard to keep my nephew out of trouble. Never more than that moment did I feel that I had failed him...Can you believe it? It was all

for nothing...

Outro

So, there you have it. I could have kept going but what's the point? You might have known what happened after...Chauncey got arrested and six months later died of inmate brutality. And as for me at the time, my job was in jeopardy. My relationship with Chauncey was destroyed as I pretended for my sake that I had not known of his corrupt nature. I had no plans on retiring at the time and so I needed the money. But I had worked hard on a deal that would have eventually gotten him out. Unfortunately, my nephew was killed in prison before my plan came into fruition. There was nothing worse for me than seeing Chauncey deny me every time I went to visit him. And I still carry the guilt trip to this day. On the bright side, at least everyone who had to be dealt with got theirs in the end. After taking care of Jake Fisher myself, I threw Ron Mercer into the waters of Coney Island where he drowned immediately. Finally, I sabotaged Luke (now known as detective Fisher) who is currently left with no means of getting to me. And last but not least, I changed my name while sipping margaritas on a tropical island. And if that isn't seen as FBI sectored then I don't know what is! Man, alotta people are just bound to lose their jobs over this. So, in signing off, let me remind you that my name is Matt Frank. The frank Matt formerly known as detective Frank Matthews. Call me crazy but I think this entire story, from beginning to end as well as myself is **"FRANKLY TWISTED."**

About The Illustrator

In discovering Alton's fine art works on his personal website, (DRAWINGREALM.weebly.com) Kevin recruited Alton in leading the art direction for many books to follow down the road for his independent publishing company – Flowered Concrete. As lead art director and artist in general, Alton is very thankful to show his talents to the world through Flowered Concrete as he plans to bring about his ideas in both visual and storytelling formats to help expand the diversity that is and will be FLOWERED CONCRETE .

About the Author

Kevin "Eleven" Anglade was born in Brooklyn but raised in the town of Jamaica, in Queens, New York City. Passions of the author include writing, reading, performance, poetry, and acting. Kevin became enthralled with his pen the moment he wrote his first short-story titled "Trouble is My Middle Name" in 2011 for a Detective Fiction class while taking course at Queensborough Community College. Kevin has been a creative writer for three years now and hopes to continue writing tales that evoke imagination and illusion but an escape for readers hoping for the next train back to the 23RD PRECINCT. As writer, publisher, or editor, Kevin hopes to fulfill the mission statement and inspire millions of youth down the road through FLOWERED CONCRETE.

Mission Statement

Flowered Concrete Publishing was established on the sixteenth day of June 2012. The purpose of its manifestation and current existence is to offer an educational platform for readers to indulge in while being entertained. We'd like to classify all of our work as Edutainment and hope that down the road the brand will affirm this notion while trying to spread positivity, growth, and insight for youth all across the nation and readers of all ages seeking something new and refreshing. Here at Flowered Concrete, we see a bright tomorrow. We distribute literature that teaches but still incorporates a platform for imagination. Hopefully, we can all go down this road together and achieve all the things that we as people and citizens want to attain. Thanks to all who made this possible, especially CreateSpace. Hopefully, this venture will inspire the next generation to get up and do whatever it is that they want in life all on their own. Waiting on someone or something is not an option. Go out and succeed in everything you do. Dream for anything, reach for everything.

Flowered Concrete is Growing Literature One Rose At A Time

ISBN-10: 148186484X

ISBN-13:978-1481864848

Other works by Flowered Concrete:

Alton Taylor's

"The Serpent Samurai"

Available to order online @ http://www.lulu.com/us/en/shop/alton-taylor/the-serpent-samurai/ebook/product-20996475.html

"You & I"

Available to order online @

http://www.lulu.com/us/en/shop/alton-taylor/you-and-i/ebook/product-21465780.html

Kevin Eleven's

"pReSSuREd": *aNotHeR hoOd sToRy*
(Mature Readers Only!) Ages 17+]

"motown, BLUES"
(A Private-Eye Original)

"The Misadventures of The Cool"
(A Haunting Short Story)

Are all available to read for free @
www.booksie.com/Kevin11

BOOK TWO

"FRANKLY TWISTED": *THE LOST FILES*

Coming SOON...

Made in the USA
Charleston, SC
17 January 2015